Gillian Cross

With illustrations by
Peter Cottrill

Barrington Stoke

First published in 2017 in Great Britain by
Barrington Stoke Ltd
18 Walker Street, Edinburgh, EH3 7LP

www.barringtonstoke.co.uk

ISBN: 978-1-78112-566-3

Printed in China by Leo

Contents

Chapter 1
It's today!

At six o'clock on Monday morning Lara woke up with a big smile on her face.

'It's today!' she thought. 'I'm going to Art Camp!'

She was almost ready. Her bag was packed. Her jeans and T-shirt and sandals were laid out on her chair, all set. She'd made her packed lunch the night before and now it was in the fridge, ready to eat on the minibus.

Lara jumped out of bed and ran to the landing. "Dad!" she shouted. "Are you up? We have to be at the pick-up place by 7 a.m."

Dad came out of his bedroom. He was yawning and he looked very sleepy, but he was wearing jeans, not his PJs. "Don't worry," he said. "I haven't forgotten."

Lara pointed at her watch. "Look at the time!" she said. "We've only got an hour. If I'm late, the minibus will go without me."

Dad grinned. "It's OK," he said, and he pulled on his hoody. "There's plenty of time to wash and have breakfast. You won't be late."

Dad was right. They didn't miss the minibus. In fact, he and Lara were the first people there – except for a tall man holding a video camera. He grinned and bounced up to them.

"Mr ... Mackenzie?" Dad said.

"Call me Mr Mac!" the man said. He beamed at Lara. "Are you looking forward to Art Camp, Lara?"

Lara nodded.

"It's going to be AMAZING!" Mr Mac said. "We'll be in a big old house, in the middle of a wood. With a brilliant Art teacher called Ana Maria. You'll be making wonderful arty things – and I'll be filming everything. I'm going to make a brilliant video of it all!"

He pointed the camera at Lara and her dad.

"You're starting the film now?" Dad said.

Mr Mac nodded. "Smile, both of you!"

Dad and Lara gave Mr Mac their best early-morning smiles. Then Ted from Lara's class came along, with his mum and their two greyhounds. Mr Mac filmed Ted as he said goodbye to the two dogs.

"Mr Mac's even more excited than you are," Dad whispered to Lara.

Lara grinned. "He loves that video camera," she said.

Ted was grinning too. "He thinks he's a hot-shot film director and we're his crew."

Lara's friend Jemma was the next to arrive. Mr Mac filmed her too. And then the minibus drove up and he got Lara and Jemma to stand beside it so he could film that too.

Dad kept looking round as more and more children appeared. "There should be another leader from the Council Outdoor team too," he muttered. "Someone called Miss Begum."

He was right. But she was the very last person to get there. Mr Mac filmed her running up the road with her suitcase bumping along behind her.

"Sorry! Sorry!" Miss Begum panted. "I turned my alarm off and went back to sleep!"

She took out her clipboard and called people's names, to make sure everyone was there. She had to call Ted's name twice, because he didn't hear the first time. He was staring up at the sky, watching the clouds.

Then they got into the minibus. Lara sat with Jemma. Ted was right at the back, next to a very tall boy called Bruno.

"Right!" Mr Mac shouted. "Let's get this show on the road!"

"Goodbye! Goodbye!" called all the mums and dads and brothers and sisters and everyone else who had been dragged out of bed at 6 a.m. to wave goodbye.

Mr Mac filmed them through the window. Then he turned the camera round and pointed it down the minibus. "Wave!" he yelled.

And he filmed as all the children waved and cheered and clapped and shouted. They were on their way!

It was a long, long journey. They stopped halfway, to eat what was left of their packed lunches. Then the minibus turned off the motorway, onto a narrow twisting road with high trees on either side. It seemed to go on and on and on.

"We'll be late!" Miss Begum said. She sounded nervous. "We're supposed to be there by 4 p.m."

"Don't panic," the driver said. "Only one more mile to go."

The road got narrower and narrower. They drove into a dark wood and then the minibus turned down a rough track rutted with holes. Everyone squealed as they went over a big bump.

"This is the middle of nowhere!" Jemma said.

At the end of the track there was a big farm gate. On the other side of the gate was a yard in front of an old white house. Mr Mac jumped out to open the gate and he filmed the minibus driving in. Then he ran ahead, into the yard, so he could film them arriving.

The driver parked outside the house. The front door opened and a tall woman drifted out. She had long red hair and she was wearing a silky patchwork dress. Lara thought she looked beautiful – exactly the way she imagined an artist would look.

"Welcome!" the woman said, and she flung her arms wide. "I'm Ana Maria. I'll be working with you this week. We're going to have a magical time, exploring the woods and making BEAUTIFUL things."

"And a film!" said Mr Mac. "I'm going to make a brilliant film of all your wonderful projects!"

Ana Maria smiled. "Let's start by looking round the house. Bring your bags and I'll show you your rooms."

The driver helped unload their bags out of the minibus. Lara grabbed hers.

"Come on!" she said to Jemma. "I can't wait to see our room."

Ana Maria took Lara and Jemma up to the very top of the house. They were sharing a tiny attic room with a little window and low, sloping ceilings. From the window they could see right into the woods.

"It's amazing!" Jemma said.

Lara nodded and grinned. "I can't wait for tomorrow!"

Chapter 2
Into the woods

In the morning, Lara opened the bedroom curtains and bent down to look out of the little window. She could see the round shape of a bird's nest in one of the trees outside. Ted was standing at the bottom of the tree.

"Hi, Ted!" Lara shouted.

She startled the birds outside the window, but Ted didn't hear her. He was staring up at the nest.

Jemma wasn't interested in the nest or in looking outside. "I'm starving!" she said. "Let's go and see what's for breakfast."

They ran down to the kitchen. Miss Begum was making slice after slice of toast and Mr Mac was boiling eggs and putting them in a row of egg cups.

Ana Maria was sitting on the table with a glass of mint tea in her hand.

"Hurry up and eat!" she called. "Then we can go out into the woods."

Lara ate her breakfast as fast as she could. So did all the others. By 8.30 a.m., everyone was ready at the front door. Ana Maria gave each of them a brown paper bag.

"These are your treasure bags," she said. "See what you can find in the woods. Don't pick anything that's still growing, but keep your eyes open for interesting things like fir cones and pretty leaves and nut shells. When we come back, you'll use them to make your first piece of art."

Off they went into the woods. Mr Mac ran backwards and forwards, filming them as they walked about and picked things up. Lara put some perfect pine cones into her bag and Jemma found a pile of empty nut shells.

Ana Maria smiled at the nut shells. "I think a squirrel's had a feast," she said. "Go on, put them in your bag!"

Soon their bags were full and they were heading back to the house. Mr Mac was still filming – of course. Miss Begum kept counting children, to make sure no one was lost.

Ana Maria laughed. "Don't *worry* so much!" she told Miss Begum. "The woods are here to explore. Relax and enjoy yourself."

When they got back to the house, Ana Maria made Miss Begum put her clipboard away. Then everyone went into the old barn beside the house. There were four big tables in there, and shelves full of paints and paper and all kinds of useful crafty things.

Ana Maria flung her arms wide. "Welcome to our workshop!" she said. "Now let's make some lovely woodland creatures."

They spent the rest of the day making squirrels and mice and moles out of all the things they'd collected from the woods. Lara made an owl and she thought all the little animals were very sweet lined up together.

But Mr Mac wasn't happy. He wandered about the barn and filmed the children as they worked, but he kept frowning.

At tea time, Ana Maria clapped her hands. "Good work, everyone!" she said. "Tomorrow we'll do some more exploring. And maybe you can make some insects – beetles and dragonflies and ladybirds. And butterflies and moths too."

Mr Mac shook his head. "Those are all too small," he said. "How can I make a brilliant BIG film out of tiny little animals? I need the children to work all together, to make something HUGE."

It was Ana Maria's turn to frown. "That's not what I planned," she said.

But Mr Mac didn't take any notice. He waved the video camera at the children. "Come on, everyone. I want some BIG ideas. What shall we make?"

No one said anything. Lara felt a bit embarrassed. But Mr Mac didn't give up.

"How about – a giant sculpture?" he said. "Of something that lives in the woods." Still no one said anything. Mr Mac pointed at

Bruno. "Come on," he said. "Choose a woodland animal."

"Um – a squirrel?" Bruno said.

"Great idea!" Mr Mac beamed at him. "Let's make a giant squirrel!"

Ana Maria shuddered, but Mr Mac was too busy thinking about the giant squirrel to take any notice.

"First of all, we'll make a wooden squirrel skeleton," he said. "And use dead leaves for its fur. And we won't make it in here in the barn. We'll build it out in the yard. Then it can be ENORMOUS!"

Ana Maria stared at him with her mouth wide open. But Mr Mac was too excited to spot the look of horror on her face.

"A giant squirrel," he said. "We'll start tomorrow!"

Chapter 3
The giant squirrel

The next day was Wednesday. As soon as breakfast was over, Mr Mac chased all the children out of the house.

"We need lots of branches!" he said. "To make a skeleton for our giant squirrel. Go into the woods and collect as many as you can."

"Only branches that are on the ground," Ana Maria called. "You mustn't break any off the trees."

"Lots of big, dead branches," said a happy Mr Mac. "That's what we want. And I'll need a saw and a hammer, so I can cut them up and nail them together."

"It all sounds very – noisy," Ana Maria whispered.

But Lara was the only person who heard her. Everyone else was heading for the woods.

An hour later, there was a heap of dead branches in the yard. Mr Mac bounced around, filming the children with his video camera.

"Pile up those branches!" he kept shouting. "We need a big heap for the squirrel's body. Bruno – you're the tallest. Put more on the top of the pile!"

"Is that safe?" Miss Begum said. She looked alarmed. "Suppose some of the branches fall? The children might get hurt."

Mr Mac waved his hand to brush her worries away. "Nonsense," he said. "It's perfectly safe."

"It looks like a bonfire," Jemma whispered to Lara.

But Lara wasn't listening. She was watching Ted as he came out of the trees. He had a branch in his hands – but he didn't bring it into the yard. He went the other way, deeper into the woods.

'That's weird,' Lara thought. 'What's he up to?'

She kept watching. After a couple of minutes, she saw Ted again, with another branch. And he went the same way as before. Away from the yard and into the woods.

What was he doing?

After that, she didn't see him again until they went into the house for lunch. Ted sat by himself while he ate his sandwiches. He was smiling a secret sort of smile.

Lara looked at him and wondered again what he was up to.

But she didn't have much time to think. Mr Mac wolfed down his lunch, very fast, and then jumped up and waved his arms around till everyone stopped talking.

"You've found lots of branches," he said. "Enough for a really huge squirrel. Now we need dead leaves. Thousands and thousands of them! Eat up your sandwiches, then get out there and start collecting. Ana Maria, please can we have some bags for the leaves?"

Ana Maria went a bit pale. But she didn't say anything. She went into the kitchen and found lots of bags.

"Into the woods!" Mr Mac shouted. "A bar of chocolate for the person who collects the most leaves!"

Jemma pulled at Lara's sleeve. "Come on!" she said. "Let's win that chocolate!"

But Lara wasn't interested in chocolate. She wanted to find out what Ted was up to. "I'm not finished yet," she muttered. "You go and start collecting. I'll come and find you in a minute."

Jemma grabbed a handful of bags and went off to look for dead leaves. Lara chewed her sandwich very slowly as she waited for Ted to move.

He did it so silently that she nearly missed him. One moment he was there on the other side of the room. The next moment – he was gone. Lara looked out of the window just in time to see him disappear into the trees. He was going a different way from everyone else.

Lara jumped up and went after him. But when she reached the trees there was no sign of him. He'd vanished.

Lara stood there for a moment and looked round, but she couldn't see him. She was just about to give up when she heard a tiny noise above her. Something was moving, high in the trees. Something – or someone. She took a step closer and looked up into the canopy of leaves arching over her head.

"Ted?" she called. "Is that you?"

For a moment there was complete silence and stillness. Then she heard Ted's voice, high above her head.

"Shhhh. It's a secret," he said. His voice was so soft Lara could only just hear him. "Please don't tell Mr Mac."

"What's a secret?" Lara said. "What have you got up there?"

"You can come up and see," Ted said. "If you promise not to tell."

"I promise," said Lara. "But – how do I get up?"

"You have to climb." Ted stuck his head out of the leaves of the huge oak tree and pointed down at the trunk. "Look, there are places to put your feet. There. And there. And there."

Lara started to climb. It was tricky at first, and it seemed a very long way up. But at last she was at the same level as Ted, who was perched on a big, wide branch.

"Is this it?" Lara said. "Is this the secret?"

Ted grinned. "No, you're not there yet. You have to climb higher. Come on."

He started to climb up and Lara followed him. At first she couldn't see anything except branches and leaves. Then her head came out into an open space in the middle of the tree – and she gasped.

Two of the tree's branches flattened out just there. In between them were lots of big bits of wood neatly tied together with rope.

"It's like a floor!" Lara said.

Ted nodded. "It *is* a floor," he said. "The floor of a tree house."

He climbed up onto the rows of wood and walked across them. Then he jumped up and down in the middle. The floor didn't even wobble.

"It's really strong," he said. "You can come up too if you like."

With great care, Lara climbed up to the tree house. Ted was right. There was lots of room for both of them and the floor felt very sturdy. Lara was impressed!

"I'm going to make a roof for it," Ted said. "And lots of other things too."

There was a fantastic view. No one could see them, because they were hidden by the leaves. But from the tree house Lara could see the house and the yard – and the giant squirrel skeleton.

"Look," Lara said. "Mr Mac's nailing the branches together. The squirrel's going to be massive."

"And horrible," said Ted. He pulled a face. "It's going to be *ugly*. Not like a real squirrel at all."

"What do you mean?" Lara said.

Ted put a finger on his lips. "Sssh," he said. "If you stay still you might see in a minute."

Lara's heart was thumping, but she sat very still. After a minute or two, Ted touched her arm and nodded to one side. And there was a squirrel, right next to them, running along a branch.

Chapter 4
A REAL squirrel

The squirrel danced towards them with its tail floating behind it. It was so light it hardly seemed to touch the branch.

"Isn't it beautiful!" Lara whispered.

Ted put his hand out, to stop her talking, but he was too late. The squirrel looked towards them and froze for a second. It stood perfectly still on the branch, then it jumped higher up into the tree and disappeared among the leaves.

"Wow!" Lara said. "That was amazing!"

"See what I mean about Mr Mac's squirrel?" said Ted. "It's not like a real one at all."

Lara looked down into the yard. Ted was right. She couldn't imagine Mr Mac's squirrel dancing along a tree branch. It was a lumpy, ugly monster. And Mr Mac was making a horrible noise as he built it. He was knocking nails into the branches with a big hammer, to hold the skeleton together.

But his noisy hammering wasn't working very well. Lara could see he was having problems with the squirrel's tail. It was a big branch with lots of smaller branches coming off it and it kept falling off the main body.

"Bruno, come here!" Mr Mac shouted. "I need you to hold the tail!"

Bruno came out of the workshop with something in his hands. "Please can I finish making my woodpecker first?" he said.

"Of course not!" Mr Mac snapped. "If you don't come NOW, this squirrel's tail will fall off."

Bruno frowned, but he took his little bird back in the workshop and went to hold the squirrel's tail. He was really tall, but he still had to stand on tiptoe to reach. He didn't look very happy.

Miss Begum didn't look happy either. She kept waving her clipboard at Mr Mac. "That's dangerous!" she called out. "PLEASE be careful!"

And then Lara spotted Ana Maria. She looked even more unhappy. She was standing in the doorway of the workshop, with her hands over her ears. And she was shaking her head at the wooden squirrel.

Mr Mac pressed on. He banged some more nails into the tail. Then he put down his hammer and picked up the video camera.

"Right! Let's get this on film!" he said. Then he shouted into the woods. "Come here, everyone! It's film time again!"

Up in the tree house, Ted looked at Lara. "We'd better go," he whispered. "Or Mr Mac might come looking for us. Remember – you promised not to tell anyone. This tree house is our secret."

"Don't worry," Lara whispered back. "I won't say a word."

They scrambled down the tree and ran back into the yard. Mr Mac waved them over to the giant squirrel.

"Stand there, with the others!" he said. "And SMILE. Remember, this is YOUR squirrel!"

Jemma was standing next to Lara. "It's not OUR squirrel," she muttered. "It's Mr Mac's squirrel. He's done all the work. I've made a caterpillar."

She held out her hand to show Lara. She'd made the caterpillar out of lots of nut shells linked together. There were tiny patterns painted on all the shells and she'd stuck on two little beads for eyes. It was gorgeous.

"I made an ant as well," Jemma said. "Ana Maria helped me work out how to do it. Look."

She held out her other hand and there was the ant. It was made of shiny black seeds, with black wire for its legs.

"That's lovely," Lara said. "You should make a whole row of them and Mr Mac could put it in the video."

Jemma shook her head. "He says it's too small." She looked sad.

They heard Mr Mac start shouting again. "Lara! Jemma! I need you over here, closer to the squirrel. Talk to each other about how you collected branches for the skeleton. Then I can film you."

Lara and Jemma went up to the squirrel. Bruno was still holding its tail up in the air.

"My arms are killing me," he groaned. "I can't take this much longer."

"*Smile!*" Mr Mac shouted, as he held up the camera.

Lara and Jemma didn't have much to say about the branches – but Mr Mac filmed them anyway. Then he looked round at all the children.

"Right," Mr Mac said. "Now it's time for the squirrel's fur. Who collected the most dead leaves? Who wins the chocolate?"

Some of children hadn't collected any leaves at all. They'd stayed in the workshop and made insects and birds and other little animals with Ana Maria. But Mr Mac was in luck – there were still lots of bags full of dead leaves. Ali had the most. He'd filled ten bags.

"Good boy!" Mr Mac said as he gave him the chocolate.

Ali grinned and started sharing it around.

"There's no time for that!" Mr Mac snapped. He looked back at the squirrel skeleton. "We need to get all these leaves fixed to the squirrel, so they look like fur. Ana Maria, can you tell us how to do that?"

"Come on!" Lara whispered to Ted, as Ana Maria and Mr Mac went to look at the squirrel. "Let's go back to the tree house."

They slipped away from the yard and they were halfway up the tree when they heard a voice calling.

"Lara?" the voice said. "Where are you going? What's up in that tree?"

"Oh no!" said Ted.

Chapter 5
The perfect place

Jemma was standing at the bottom of the tree, peering up at them.

Ted groaned. "Now she'll tell Mr Mac."

"No she won't," Lara said. She leaned out of the tree and called down to Jemma. "Climb up here and you'll see something wonderful. But be *quiet*."

Jemma scrambled up the tree. When she saw the tree house, her mouth fell open. "Wow!" she said. "WOW! That's amazing." She took the caterpillar and the ant out of her pocket and pretended to show them the tree house. "Look," she said to them. "Isn't it great up here? It would be a good home for you."

She put the caterpillar onto a high branch at one side of the tree house. Then she put the ant on the other side. They looked almost real, glinting among the leaves.

"It would be a good home for my little birds too," Ted muttered. "Wait here. I'm going to get them."

He climbed down the tree and slipped into the yard. Mr Mac was still talking to Ana Maria about leaves for the squirrel's fur. He didn't notice Ted creeping across to the workshop.

Jemma was looking down from the tree house. "Ted's an expert at being quiet," she said.

"He's an expert at lots of things," said Lara. "He made this tree house all by himself."

Jemma looked round. "It's perfect," she said. "Just the right home for my caterpillar and my ant."

"Yes," said Lara. "And think of all other creatures in the workshop. All those birds and butterflies and insects people were making – till Mr Mac said we had to do that stupid squirrel instead."

"I know!" said Jemma. "Wouldn't it be lovely if they were all up here – they'd look brilliant."

"We could make strange flowers too," Lara said. "And creepers – with weird-coloured fruits and odd-shaped leaves. This could be such a magical place. Only – I don't know if Ted would like it if we filled up his tree house."

"I'd love it!" Ted's voice said, from just below them.

Lara and Jemma were so busy talking that they hadn't noticed Ted creeping back across the yard. He was already halfway up the tree. When he scrambled into the tree house, they saw he had a bag on his back.

"I've brought all my birds," he said. "Let's put them on the branches."

He began to place his birds among the leaves, twisting the wire of their tiny claws so they gripped the branches. He was still doing this when there was a sound from lower down the tree.

Someone else was climbing up.

"Where are you, Ted?" a voice said.

"Wait for us," said a different voice.

Then two heads popped up past the branches. It was the twins, Sally and Dan. Sally was holding a little grey bird with a bunch of bright tail feathers. She had painted the feathers purple and stuck glitter all over them. Dan had a long, long snake, made of conkers strung together.

"What are you doing here?" said Lara.

Dan grinned. "We saw Ted taking his birds out of the workshop," he said.

"So we followed him," said Sally. "To see what he was doing."

They both scrambled into the tree house and looked around.

"It's amazing," Sally whispered. "And your birds look fantastic, Ted. Can I put mine here too?"

"And my snake?" said Dan.

"They'll look good up here," Jemma said. "We're going to make some creepers too, to wind round the branches. And flowers."

"You'd better hurry then," said Sally. "It's Wednesday afternoon and we're going home on Friday. There's only one more day left for making things."

"We'd have lots of time," said Lara. "If it wasn't for that squirrel."

They all groaned and looked down into the yard. Poor Bruno was still holding up the giant squirrel's tail, and Mr Mac had just finished hammering. He turned round and started calling out.

"Where IS everyone? It's time to start on the squirrel's fur. There's only one more day after today! Miss Begum, please go and fetch people out of the wood."

"Hurry!" Ted said. "We don't want her to find our tree house. Let's get back to the yard."

They left all their creatures and climbed down the oak tree as fast as they could. Before

Miss Begum could start hunting for them, they were in the yard.

Now Mr Mac had a big piece of netting. He was trying to work out a way to fix the dead leaves to the net. But the leaves were too dry and they kept crumbling into dust.

Ana Maria was watching. "It would be easier with coloured paper instead of leaves," she said.

Mr Mac looked cross. "That won't fit the film," he muttered. "I've taken lots of shots of the children collecting branches and leaves. The squirrel has to be made out of those."

He turned his back on Ana Maria and called out again. "Come on, everyone. Come and fix the leaves to this net!"

"Me too?" Bruno said. He was still holding up the squirrel's tail and he looked very, VERY tired, as if his arms might give way at any moment.

"No!" Mr Mac shouted. "You mustn't move. You have to keep holding –"

But he didn't finish what he was saying – because all of a sudden there was a loud CRACK!

And Bruno wailed, "NO!!!"

Chapter 6
Disaster!

There was a loud CRUNCH! And a creaking, splitting noise.

"Quick, Bruno!" Miss Begum yelled. "Get out of the way! RUN!"

Bruno let go of the squirrel's tail and raced towards the others. He was just in time. With an ear-splitting CRACK! the huge tail swung forward, pulling the rest of the giant sculpture with it. The squirrel skeleton toppled over, hit the ground and broke into a million pieces. Branches snapped and nails flew through the air.

"Cover your eyes!" Miss Begum shouted.

They all did as they were told until everything was still. Then they looked at the giant squirrel again.

It was a total ruin. There was nothing left except a mess of broken branches.

Mr Mac stared at it in horror. "What now?" he said.

"We could – um – video what's happened," Miss Begum suggested.

"And end my film with a disaster? Never!" Mr Mac walked across to the ruins of the squirrel. "Maybe we can fix it."

But everyone could see that was impossible. They would have to start from scratch and there wasn't time.

"So we haven't made anything big this week," Miss Begum said. She looked very sad.

There was a terrible silence. Then Ana Maria stepped forward. "There is something," she said, in her quiet voice. "Something beautiful. And the children made it all by themselves."

"Where?" said Mr Mac. He looked round the yard. "I can't see anything."

"I think it's a secret," Ana Maria said. "But – maybe the people who made it will tell you."

She looked across at Lara and Ted – and Lara understood. "Ana Maria's talking about the tree house," she whispered to Ted. "She wants to show it to Mr Mac."

Ted looked behind him, into the woods. Then he looked round at Mr Mac. "Follow me," he said. "Everyone follow me."

He led everyone into the woods, to the bottom of the big oak tree. "It's up there," he said.

"In the tree?" Miss Begum looked shocked. "But that's DANGEROUS."

"No it's not," Ted said. "Come and see."

Before Miss Begum could answer, he started climbing.

"Come back!" Miss Begum called. But Ted went on climbing – so she started following him. And Mr Mac was close behind her.

"What's up there?" said Bruno. "Where are they going?"

Lara smiled. "It's a tree house," she said. "Ted made it. And we've put our little creatures up there."

"We want to make flowers and creepers too," said Jemma. "But we're not sure how."

Ana Maria laughed. "I'll help you!" she said. She sounded happy again. "Use the net with the dead leaves fixed to it. If you weave in some ivy, you can add flowers made of coloured paper. That will look fabulous."

"Can I put my woodpecker model up there?" Bruno said.

"Yes," said Lara. "There's lots of room – space for all the creatures we've made."

"And Mr Mac can film it!" said Jemma.

Just then Mr Mac climbed down the tree. He'd heard what Jemma said and he shook his head. "It's too late," he said. "Your tree house is brilliant, but I can't film you building it."

"Yes, you can!" said Lara. "Remember how you filmed us collecting branches? Ted used some of those for the tree house."

"And you filmed us making little animals," said Jemma. "They're up in the tree house now."

"And we're going to use the net with the dead leaves," said Bruno.

Ted popped his head out of the tree. "You can film us climbing up here with our little animals."

"And making paper flowers," Ana Maria said. "And collecting ivy. And –"

"We're your film crew," said Lara. "We'll make it work!"

By now Mr Mac was bouncing about, looking excited again. "Yes!" he said. "We'll do it together!"

Miss Begum climbed down the tree – very VERY carefully. When she was standing on the ground, she smiled round at all the children.

"It's a very safe tree house," she said. "You can all put your little animals up there tomorrow."

"And then you can look for ivy in the wood," said Ana Maria. "And make flowers for the net."

"Tomorrow's going to be a busy day!" said Lara.

Chapter 7
Starring – the Film Crew!

Next morning they were all up before 7 a.m. And they worked all day, collecting ivy, making flowers and carrying things up the tree.

They only stopped for a few minutes for lunch and, by tea time, there were creepers and flowers all over the tree, and wonderful, bright little creatures on all the branches. The tree house looked magical.

But the yard outside the house was a terrible mess.

"We must clear up all these broken branches," Miss Begum said to Ana Maria.

But Ana Maria shook her head. "I've got a better idea. Let's make a bonfire and sit round it while we eat our supper."

"Yay!" said Bruno. "Let's do it NOW!"

"Wait till it's dark," said Mr Mac. "The bonfire will be more fun then. And there's something I need to do first."

He disappeared into the house with his camera. Miss Begum and the children piled all the broken branches into one massive heap. It was going to be a great bonfire.

By 9 p.m. it was dark. Miss Begum lit the fire and they all sat round it and ate their supper. Then Ana Maria handed out marshmallows to toast in the flames.

"This is perfect," said Ted, as he held a stick of marshmallows towards the fire.

"It's just about to get even better," said Mr Mac. "Turn round, everyone."

They all turned towards the house. Mr Mac was standing there with his projector.

"There's our cinema screen," said Mr Mac, and he pointed to the white wall at the side of the house. "Now watch this!"

Mr Mac switched on the projector with a flourish – and there were their faces up on the wall. Very, very large.

"Yay!" said Lara. "We're the stars!"

They sat round the fire and watched the story of their week at Art Camp, from the moment they got on the minibus until the moment the tree house was finished. Mr Mac

had added some music and funny captions – it was a great film.

"There's only one thing missing," Lara whispered to Ted. "There are no pictures of Mr Mac's squirrel."

"Maybe he's trying to forget it," Ted whispered back.

But he was wrong. At the very end, after all their names had scrolled past, the screen turned purple, with giant golden letters spread across it –

THIS FILM WAS BROUGHT TO YOU BY
GIANT SQUIRREL PRODUCTIONS

And Mr Mac took a bow as the Film Crew all clapped and cheered.

Our books are tested
for children and young people by
children and young people.

Thanks to everyone who consulted on
a manuscript for their time and effort in
helping us to make our books better
for our readers.